ASPEN—
WHERE ARE YOU?

ALL ROADS LEAD TO HOME

TAMMY LANE

AuthorHouse™
1663 Liberty Drive
Bloomington, IN 47403
www.authorhouse.com
Phone: 1 (800) 839-8640

Published by AuthorHouse 10/04/2018

ISBN: 978-1-5462-6040-0 (sc)
ISBN: 978-1-5462-6039-4 (e)

Library of Congress Control Number: 2018911066

Print information available on the last page.

author**HOUSE**®

WHERE IS
ASPEN?

NARRATOR'S VERSION

BY:

TAMMY LANE

*Dedicated to Uncle Kevin and Cousin Kali
and anyone who has ever lost a pet.*

INTRODUCTION

The Story of Aspen, a black Australian-Rottweiler mix breed dog who took an adventurous ride and finds herself in a serious <mark>predicament</mark>. Can she survive this strange unforeseen situation?

IN THEY GO

"Come on Kino, Chye, and Aspen! Let's go to the farm," <mark>coaxed</mark> Kevin. In jump the three active, excited dogs who love to go for rides and, even better, run free on the family farm.

ALL ABOUT THE CANINES

Kino is a Rottweiler, Mastiff, Pit Bull Mixed breed, while Chye is a beagle, lab mixed breed. Both dogs are very active and conform to change well. They follow Kevin's lead and perk up their little-pointed ears as they leap into the family van. Aspen, on the other hand, is a bit conservative and apprehensive. She requires a little more encouragement to take on the journey. She only resides with Kevin when his daughter Kali is home from college. She can be easily spooked by random noises and unfamiliar places which makes her a bit more unsure at times. But once she's on the road, seems happy to join in on the adventure.

PLEADING WITH DAD

"No Dad," replies Kali. "Don't take Aspen! You know how she can be." Aspen happens to be Kali's dog. She has had her for three years and adopted her from an animal shelter when she was about six months old. Kali is Kevin's 21-year-old daughter who is finishing her last year of college.

DAD TAKES OFF

"Oh, come on Kal, Aspen needs to get some exercise too. She'll be fine!" bellows Kevin. Without <mark>heeding</mark> his daughter's advice, off they go!

FARM FUN

Upon arriving at the farm, Kino and Chye excitedly hop out of the van and take off for the vast fields that await and enjoy the new sense of freedom on the many acres before them. The dogs take off for the fields in search of new smells or wherever their noses take them. It soon appears they have spotted a rabbit and the chase is on.

UNSURE OF THIS ADVENTURE

Aspen, on the other hand, slowly exits the van and peers around before taking the next step of exploring her new surroundings. She finally decides it must be ok and follows the other two canines as they explore a rabbit hole. But, after she discovers that Kino, the black lab, has **monopolized** the hole, Aspen decides to wander off to explore something else.

SPOOKED

Her nose takes her deeper into the woods with the scent of something different. After a few minutes of exploring, Aspen hears a SNAP and a CRACK and she is instantly spooked. As she looks up, she sees a falling branch headed right at her. She tries to turn and run, but something has snagged her tail and she starts to panic. She pulls with all her might and narrowly escapes unscathed by the branch. She is clearly startled though, and as she makes her escape, runs as far and as fast as she can. She sees a nearby truck and decides to take cover there. Oh no! The door is closed. She instantly decides to take cover underneath the truck. Whew! Safe at last.

HOMEBOUND

After a few hours of visiting the farm and accomplishing some needed chores, it's time to gather the furry friends and set out for home.

Upon Kevin's whistle, Chye and Kino come racing back to the van, ready to end their farm fun. Kino hops into the van wagging her tail rapidly. Chye follows, panting heavily, as she slobbers all over the back of the seat.

MISSING

"Now, just one more," murmurs Kevin. "Aspen, here girl, where are you? Are you ready to go home?"

Well, after several minutes of calling her and no response, Kevin starts to stress a little. *Where could she be?* He contemplates. She was just here a little while ago. "Aspen, come on girl! Where are you?"

WHERE IS SHE?

As Kevin starts to weigh his options, he forcefully calls her once again. Still... no Aspen. After an hour of calling and walking the perimeter of the property, Aspen remains unfound.

DREADED PHONE CALL

After Kevin has exhausted all of his options, he decides it's time to call Kali and break the news about her missing dog. He is pretty sure she isn't going to be happy with him! Dread sinks in as he picks up his phone, goes to his favorites and searches her name. "Kal'?" Kevin speaks with apprehension. "Aspen is missing....!" I've been searching for her for a while now and she isn't coming when I call her."

UNHAPPY DAUGHTER

"Dad, what do you mean she is missing?" "I told you not to take her to the farm," Kali screams into the phone as anxiety overwhelms her.

"Don't worry Kal, we will find her. She can't be far," Kevin says as he tries to calm his upset daughter.

THE SEARCH IS ON

Several family members and a few friends gathered to perform a search of the farm. Unfortunately, after hours of searching, night sets in and the family is forced to call it a night. Having to leave without her precious Aspen is devastating to Kali.

UNSUCCESSFUL SEARCH

"Let's try again in the morning Kal. Don't worry, we'll find her." Kevin says as they head for home. *But will we?* He wonders. *Where could she be? Did something get her? I guess she is* ==skittish==. *I wish I had left her at home.*

A NEW DAY

The sun is up and its now Sunday morning. Time to get ready for church. The search will continue later. Prayers will be needed for the safe return of sweet Aspen.

PLEA FOR HELP

With the awesome advancements of technology, Kali puts a plea on Facebook for the local community to keep an eye out for Aspen. She even includes a $300.00 reward.

EXPANDED SEARCH

The search continues, only this time they expand it beyond the farm and look along highways and down gravel roads. She must be somewhere. Dogs are keen sniffers and her nose must have taken her after something of interest. Why else wouldn't she have come when called. *She was out of range, right?* wonders Kali.

STILL MISSING

After a long day of searching, still no Aspen. Dread begins to set in, but Kali isn't ready to give up. As Monday morning approaches, Kali has decided to expand the search even further. Her cousin Karinne and her friend Garrett join in on the search. Karinne knows the feeling of having a missing dog. Just a few months before, her Siberian Husky took a hiatus for nine agonizing hours. That is nothing compared to day three of Aspen's disappearance though.

NEW HELP ARRIVES

As the search continues more friends and family pitch in. The entire community is on the lookout. Unfortunately, each day brings more lost hope of finding sweet Aspen. Maybe she's injured somewhere, maybe someone picked her up and took her home thinking she was abandoned. Who knows, but more frustration and anxiety sink in for Kali, Kevin, and her extended family. Kali's Aunt Cheri decides to add another $500 to the reward of Aspen's finding. The reward now totals $800.

PLEASE HELP

    Wednesday morning has arrived. It's been since Saturday that Aspen has been last seen. Kali makes more pleas for help keeping her Facebook friends updated on places they've looked and possibilities of where people should continue to search.

    A few people have claimed they spotted two dogs along Frene Creek Road. Kevin and Kali instantly drive that direction, but to no avail.

FALSE ALARM

Neither of the dogs spotted is Aspen. The moments of brief hope fade into another letdown. Wednesday continues to be another failed attempt at finding Aspen.

It's now Thursday, and all eyes are still peeled. Friends who own horses decide to ride up and down gravel roads in search of Kali's beloved Aspen.

It seems another day is winding down with no success.

It's five o'clock and the sun will be down within a couple of hours. It looks like hope is running out.

AWAITED PHONE CALL

At five thirty p.m., Kali's phone rings and a familiar voice is on the other end.

"Kali, you won't believe this," Noah says," but we think we found your dog." Kali's heart is racing at this point and she instantly wonders if the news will be all good.

"Is she alive?" Kali blurts out.

COULD IT BE?

"Well," Noah replies, "we think so. We see her but haven't been able to get her out yet. She appears to be stuck under the back of the fertilizer truck we started working on. When we (Noah and Kali's cousin Jeff) went to start it, it choked up, so we popped the hood. Upon looking down, we can see a black dog. So we went to the back and there she was. Kali, this is the truck your dad asked us to service last week when he was on the farm. The crazy thing is, we drove it to Montgomery where our shop is. That's at least 30 miles from the farm."

ROAD TRIP

Kali instantly says, "I'll be right there!" As she gets into her car, she calls her dad and they take the thirty mile trip to Montgomery to see if it is Aspen and if she is OK.

KEEPING FAITH

The entire ride there, Kali and her dad talk about how this could have happened and not to be too discouraged as to their findings or if it is even Aspen. I mean she has had to be trapped under that hood for five nights and six days with no food and no water. What condition would she be in? Kali can't seem to get there fast enough as she steps on the accelerator and prays it is Aspen and that she is alive and well.

WHAT A MESS!

Upon arrival to the mechanic's shop, Kali can see truck parts laying all over the place. They are just getting ready to pull out the black dog that is now free from its enclosure. Kali runs over and sees that it appears to be Aspen. As she calls her name, a faint whimper is heard.

TEARS OF JOY!

Oh thank goodness, she is alive. You can see that Aspen recognizes Kali's voice and attempts to communicate her well-being. However, Kali instantly notices that Aspen is injured and needs immediate medical attention. Her backside is burned so badly that she has no hair left and the skin is red and raw. It looks to be painful. The motor must have burnt her when it was en route to the mechanic's shop.

FREE AT LAST!

How did she ever manage to take a thirty-mile trip trapped under a hood with its engine getting increasingly hotter causing such severe burns? And not only that, but the truck was moved several days ago. Poor Aspen has had to endure this pain for some time now.

TIME TO GO

Kali quickly, but carefully, picks up Aspen and carries her to the car. She places her on the back seat and cuddles with her on the ride home while Kevin drives. She begins placing calls to the local vet office so that she can be treated. Her condition is still unknown. The veterinarian on call agrees to meet her at the office. The time is now around 7:00 p.m.

FOUND—BUT NOT OUT OF THE WOODS

As Aspen is being evaluated, Kali places a message on Facebook announcing that her beloved Aspen has been Found at last. She also says she will give updates on her condition as they come forward.

It's a bittersweet moment for all. Aspen is found, but she is also badly injured.

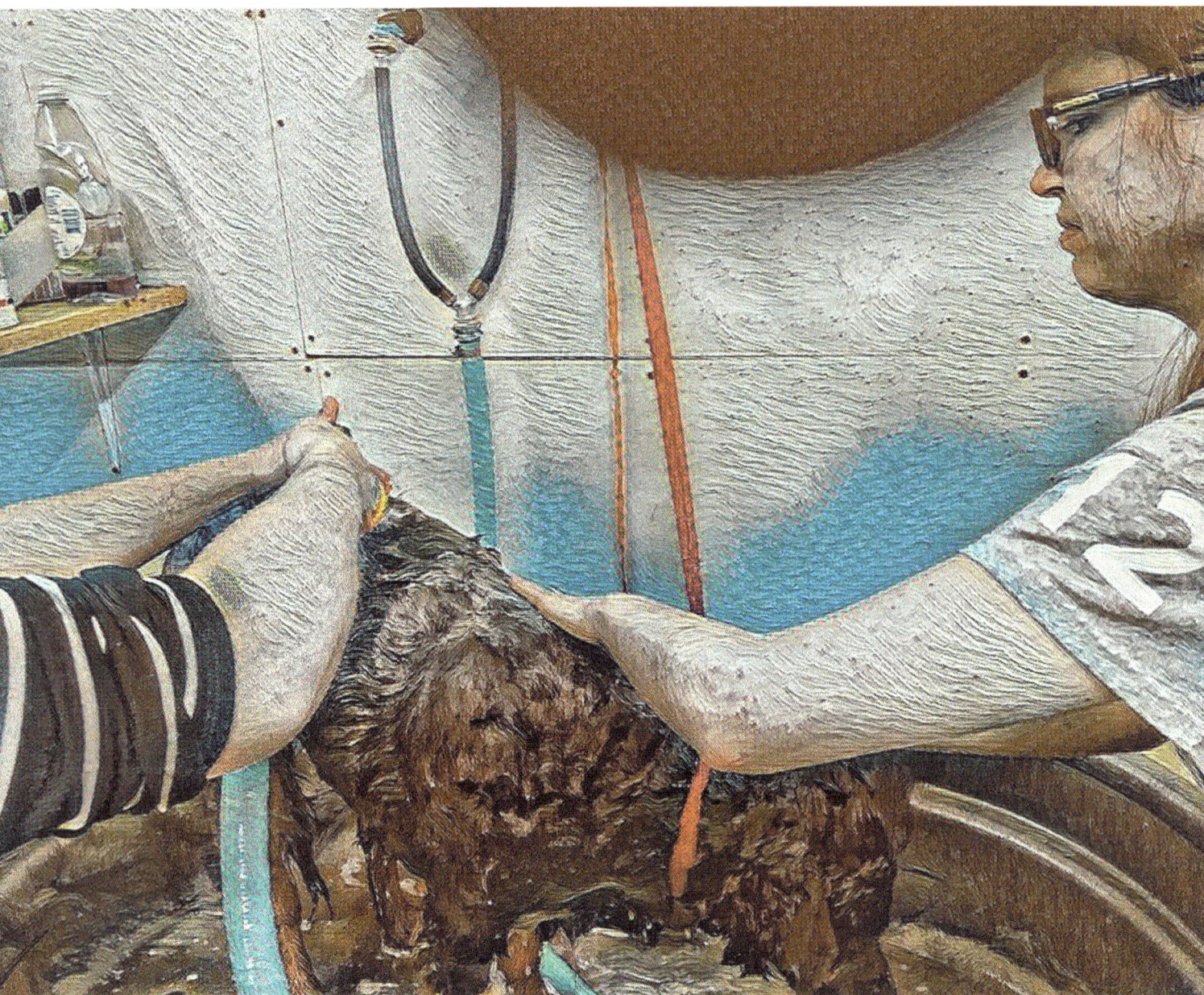

TREATING ASPEN

Upon arrival at the veterinarian office, Aspen is <mark>evaluated</mark> and is found to be severely <mark>dehydrated</mark>. Her burns are serious and she will require a procedure called debridement to clean and treat the wounds. Aspen will need to remain at the animal hospital overnight. She will need IV fluids and antibiotic medicine to hydrate her and treat the wound for infection.

SAFELY HOME

It takes several months for Aspen to fully recover from her burns, but she is happy to be home with her Kal and Kal's family is relieved she has been found. With love and nurturing, wounds can heal and friendships renewed.

LESSON LEARNED

Needless to say, when Kevin calls for the dogs to go to the farm, Aspen is allowed to stay behind, where she feels secure from all the things that make her skittish.

GLOSSARY

Apprehensive - unsure

Avail - help or benefit

Coaxed - encouraged

Cohabiters - to live with others

Conform - Adjust

Contemplates - wonders, trying to make a decision based on options available.

Dehydrated - lack of water in your body

Evaluated - looked at carefully and thoroughly

Heeding - listening to

Hiatus - break from work

Monopolized - take control of by oneself

Predicament - "in a pickle" or bad situation

Reside - live or stay with

Saunter - to walk slowly, a leisurely stroll

Skittish - easily scared, unsure, nervous, jumpy

Unscathed - unharmed, not injured, safe

PLEASE FIND ME, I'M RIGHT HERE!

Will I Be Saved?

Aspen takes an adventurous ride and finds herself in a serious predicament. Will anyone find her before her fate is changed forever?

TAMMY LANE

Adventure, Animals, Lesson Learned

PLEASE FIND ME, I'M RIGHT HERE!

By: Tammy Lane

"Aspen, come here girl!" It's my human owner's father calling me. Yep, I live with him when my owner Kali is home from college. He's a friendly old guy with a big personality. *I wonder what he wants now?* He usually feeds me goodies if he has any left from his plate. I can't wait to see what tasty treat I'm going to get.

"There you are Aspen! Hey girl, we are going to go for a ride to the farm," announces my human grandpa.

What? Wait, I don't like the farm. It's too big and there are too many noises I don't like. I mean, I like fresh clean air, but what if there are bears there? I don't like bears.

I can hear my human grandpa on the phone with my human Mom, Kali.

"Hey Kal, I'm taking the dogs to the farm for a bit," beams gramps.

When he says dogs, that also means the other canines I **reside** with when I am home from college. We have been **cohabiters,** which means we live in the same house, since my Mom, Kal adopted me from the pound. I was about six months old I guess.

Anyway, their names are Chye and Kino. They belong to my human Aunt Allison and my human grandparents Kevin and Cara.

I can hear Kali through the phone, I mean, we dogs' have a great sense of hearing.

Whew, I can hear her say, "No Dad, Aspen doesn't like the farm! There are too many things she is skittish about. It stresses her out!"

Awesome.... I am off the hook. I love how my Kali knows me so well, she is an awesome protector.

"Oh Kal, she'll be fine. She will love it out there. She can stick with Chye and Kino. They will keep her grounded," pipes gramps.

"But Dad," I hear Kali say, "You don't know her like I do."

"It'll be fine Kal," repeats gramps. "See you later."

Oh NO! He isn't going to listen to her. He's going to make me go with them.

"All right, canine crew, let's get out of here," beams Grandpa Kev. "Jump in!"

But, I don't respond. I just stand there watching my dog family jump right up in that humongous, dark green van and sit anxiously for the chance to take on a new adventure.

"Aspen, come on girl. Let's go. You'll love it." pleads Gramps.

Will I? Hmmm... maybe it won't be so bad. I mean, what could go wrong, right? I am brave and I am smart. I can fight off any bears or squirrels I may encounter. And it's obvious my human Kevin isn't going to leave without me. He can be pretty persistent.

I hesitate once more looking back at my safe haven. I admire my cozy bed and warm house with secure walls, which keep the outside world from getting me.

However, I try to be positive as I wag my tail, to show him I can do this, and jump in with the others. Off we go!

"We are here, kids!" Ha-ha! That's what Kevin likes to call us. I mean, we are like kids sometimes... as we need to be cared for in much the same way as someone's child. Consequently, we need to be fed and watered every day. We need a warm place to sleep. We also need to be groomed on a regular basis as we can get pretty smelly at times. And we need our vaccinations and shots just like babies and kids. Most importantly, we need to be showered with love. We are loyal companions.

Have you ever heard the phrase, "A dog is a man's best friend?" That's me. Kali is my best friend and I am hers.

I LOVE MY KALI!

Out jump Kino and Chye, wagging their tails happily, as if they just entered Disney World! I mean, this is their paradise. They see farm tractors to ride on and hay wagons to dodge. I, on the other hand, slowly step off the van's running board as I peer around the corner inspecting the area for bears.

Whew! It appears the coast is clear.

I can see that Chye and Kino are running through some hay fields chasing a rabbit. Well, if that doesn't look like fun! Maybe I will join in on the adventure. Here I go, …. Rabbit, where are you? I see a hole in the ground. Maybe he dodged my friends and went into his burrow. I smell something. Yes, it must be a rabbit. Just as I stick my nose in the dirt, here comes Chye, who has more hunting blood in her than me. I mean, she has natural hunting skills as her breed is a Labrador Retriever. Quickly, she starts digging out more dirt, in search of the little cotton ball tail I just witnessed scurry across the field and smell below the earth.

Maybe I'll start to explore someplace else. I mean, I can't compete with a hunting dog anyway. As I **saunter** away, I decide farm life isn't so bad. I do enjoy the interesting smells here. I'll just explore these woods nearby and see what else this new found world has out here. My nose has spotted a new smell, hmm what could that be?

Wait, I hear something…...it sounds like ……. **Crack, Snap** ……. I decide to look up and oh no…. it's headed my way…. right for me. Run, I tell myself. RUN! Suddenly, my legs become wobbly. My tail, something has my tail! It is snagged on something. A bear, it must be a bear! Its claws are gripping me hard. I have to escape! I am going to get smashed if I don't get away. I claw the ground as hard as I can and pull my tail from the grasp of my predator…*Run! Run! Run!* I tell myself. Save yourself. But where can I hide? I see nothing but a truck ahead. *There, I'll go there and hide inside.* But, the door is closed, *now what?* Underneath I go and find a spot on top of a big metal object. I'll just wedge myself in here, and then nothing will get me. *Whew! Safe at last.*

After some time, I decide that maybe it's safe to leave my hiding place. It was easy getting up here so I'll just jump down now. As I start to crawl out of there, I find myself in a **predicament**. I appear to be stuck. I can't move.

What? You've got to be kidding me!

Meanwhile, Grandpa Kevin decides it's time to head for home and he starts to call his canine friends. Chye and Kino readily run to the truck as they are eager to head home. But, *where is Aspen,* Kevin wonders, as he walks the perimeter of the property in search of sweet Aspen. After an hour of calling and calling, Kevin decides to call Kali and the search party starts.

I wonder how long I've been here, Aspen wonders... I mean, I could hear my name ...someone must be looking for me. I am guessing they can't hear my whimpers. I am trying to be as loud as I can, but my bark isn't reaching their ears. *Please look under the truck, I'm right here.* But, I continue to hear my name in the distance. They must think...., if I were nearby, I would obviously come running. I mean, I would, but I'm stuck! *Oh, I... want to go home. I hate the farm. I never wanted to come in the first place. Someone please find me.*

The hours continue to pass, and the sun goes down. It's getting darker and cooler. I hear no more voices calling my name. *They gave up on me. How could they leave me here stuck under this truck? They'll come back, I know it. Kali would never give up on me.* She is my protector and I love her. I know she loves me too.

The sun is now coming up, as I can see the light of day shine, as a shadow appears beneath me. *Ok, it's a new day. My owners will come back for me. They know I have to be here, right?*

I can hear farm equipment in the distance as the daily routine of the farm comes to life. It seems to be getting louder. Oh good, it's getting closer. Someone is coming for me. I whimper, but the loud machine out does my cries. A man's voice is talking. He must be on a phone because I only hear one voice. I feel the truck door open and then abruptly slam shut. There is a rumbling behind me and a shaking sensation. I feel like my body is vibrating. *What is happening?* The ground beneath me is moving. The truck is in motion. It's leaving, and I'm stuck underneath.

52

Minutes tick by and my location continues to change. We are now on a gravel road. It must be the gravel road we took to get here. I remember feeling these bumps before, only now my nose is mere inches from those rocks and I'm staring at what seems to be a movie reel in motion. I feel like I'm in a race, only my legs aren't running it. The truck is. I can't look down; the rushing of the road is making me feel dizzy. The minutes seem to be never ending. We are now on a highway as the rocky feeling has subsided and a smoother transition takes place. But, now I am experiencing a new problem as the speed of the vehicle is picking up. My stomach is queasy; I wish I could puke. OUCH! Something is getting hot.

My back end is warming quickly. I feel like the hair on my back end is burning off. I wish I could move. The heat continues to char me. My body is still stuck. I am wedged like lunch meat beneath two slices of bread, and I am being toasted. *When is this trip going to end? Are we there yet?* Wherever there is. I don't know how much longer I can endure this treacherous heat. My skin feels like it's badly burned.

   Finally, the truck is slowing down, and we are turning onto a new type of gravel. We must be where we were headed to. Our final destination, I hope. With any luck, I can alert someone that I am under this beast of a truck, which happens to have a fire pit attached. My ears are ringing from the loud motor I've been attached to. My hearing isn't working. The truck has come to a complete stop. *Is there anyone there?* I can't hear them. I try to bark, but I'm not sure if anything is coming out. I can't even hear myself. My back end has become unbearably burnt. The pain is worsening. *I've got to get out of here.*

Hours pass, I mean I'm guessing so, because the light of day is fading once more. I'm still stuck on this metal bench. *Isn't anyone looking for me? Where is my Kali? Gosh, I miss her so much. Please find me Kali. I hate the farm. My back hurts.*

It's dark now. The only positive thing that has happened in the last few hours is the fact that the fire pit stopped burning me. *I want to go home. I don't like it here.* Where is here? My ears can hear better now. But they only hear crickets as the night sets in. My back still stings as it rubs against the metal thing I am stuck in. Oh, I wish I'd stayed with Kino and Chye as they chased the rabbit and tried to dig it out of its burrow. *Why can't I be brave like them?*

Seconds lead to minutes and minutes tick to hours. Daylight sets in once again as hours slumber by. *What day is this,* I wonder. We went to the farm on the day before my human family dresses nicely and goes to church. I know, because they are home and don't leave for their work.

I'm getting extremely thirsty now. I wish I could get a drink. My belly is starting to make strange noises as I think about the yummy treats I get from my Kali. She takes such good care of me. Grandpa Kevin should have listened to her. She knows me better. *I am not brave. My back hurts. I want to go home. I hate the farm.*

What? You have got to be kidding me. The air is getting increasingly colder. The ground is turning white. It is snowing! But, it is April, and Spring is here, that's why we went to the farm, to enjoy a nice warm day.

Isn't anyone looking for me? Why am I still here? They should have found me by now. I haven't heard human voices for a while. Where is everyone? *Am I going to die in the metal box that has entrapped me for days now? How many days.... I lost track. I am thirsty.* Starvation has definitely set in now as hunger pains consume me. My skin is burning still. I can't see behind me, but I don't think I have any fur left on my behind. It feels raw and unprotected. *Kali, please find me. I miss you. Someone, anyone, please find me.*

The sun is rising again. *Am I still stuck in this box? Am I dreaming? Did I ever go to sleep?* I must have, this is just a dream. Wait, I can't move. I am thirsty. I am still hungry. I can envision my food container now. My behind still hurts. It isn't a dream. I've been abandoned for yet another night. I am going to die here. No one knows where to look. Of course they don't. Who would look under the hood of a truck for a lost dog? Dogs don't get scared enough to do such a thing.

Now cats…., that's another story. This is definitely what a cat would do. They are small and can squeeze in tight spaces. *I am not brave.* Why did Kevin insist I go to the farm? Kal was right, I am **skittish**. I get stressed easily. *I hate the farm. I want to go home. Kali, please find me. Someone, anyone, please find me!*

This is my yummy food container. I am so very hungry!

I am losing hope. I feel as if I can't take another day in this tight space, with my fur gone and my raw skin exposed. Night has fallen once again. Another day with no human voices. Another day with no food or water. Another day of loneliness and pain. I want to go home to my Kal. But, I feel as if I may be getting a new home soon. Maybe doggie heaven isn't so bad. I mean, no more pain, no more hunger, and no more tight spaces entrapping my aching body. *Yes...., heaven sounds like a nice place to be.* If no one finds me soon, I'll go there. I will smile and wait for a new adventure. I will miss my Kal though. I hope she misses me too. Maybe she gave up. Who knows. *I hate the farm.*

I am not sure what day it is, but I think I hear voices. Am I already in doggie heaven? Are these voices in my new home? They must be. Who would ever look for a dog trapped under the hood of a truck? The voices appear to be getting louder. My dream is becoming more vivid. Oh, how I yearned to hear voices upon my rescue. But this will have to do. *I am in doggie heaven now.* My new adventure is starting.

"I can't get the truck started! Let's take a look under the hood and see what's up, " pipes Jeff. Jeff is the mechanic who works on the farm equipment.

Jeff? ...., I know of a Jeff. What's he doing in doggie heaven?

"Oh my gosh, Larry, come here and take a look. Is this the dog that Kali has been looking for all week?" remarks Jeff.

Why did they find me now? I am already in doggie heaven.... embarking on...... aren't I?

"Sure looks like it to me," Larry insists. "Let me make a call to Kali and tell her Aspen's been found. This is the great news she's been wanting to hear."

This is the truck I took cover in, and then became stuck.
Jeff is looking in the back to see if he can find me.

So Kali never gave up on me...I knew she wouldn't. She loves me and I loved her. *But I am in doggie heaven now.*

But why do I still hear the human voices? Are they trying to get me out? Wait...., I feel something. Pain? Yes, I still feel pain. Are you supposed to be in pain if you are in heaven? I heard the humans talking once and they said heaven is a place of eternal life, free of pain and suffering. Then why do I still feel pain? *Am I not dead?*

Credit to www.jimwarren.com

I hear the voices say, "I think she is still alive. Let's get her out, and fast." But how? I think they have to take the truck pieces off before I will be able to escape the metal enclosure. I am alive. Barely though, as I only hear bits and pieces of what they are doing before I realize I am free of the metal contraption that held me so close.

It must have taken them some time to free me, because by the time I was out, Kali was there crying with tears of joy. She gasped at the sight of me and rushed me to the veterinarian. I tried to lick her, but my tongue was knotted from lack of water and my throat was scratchy. I could no longer bark to show my appreciation of saving me.

Oh, the taste of sweet water.

It must have been after veterinarian hours because they had to reopen the office to treat me. It turns out, I was severely **dehydrated**, I suffered third degree burns on my behind, and infection was setting in. I was treated with an IV bag of fluids to rehydrate me and an antibiotic to fight off infection. Of course, I was never so glad to taste sweet water on my tongue. I lapped up the water to soothe my throat and a smile crossed my face because I could kiss my Kali with my slobbery wet tongue once again.

I also had to have several procedures to repair my burned skin. I had to stay at the doggie hospital overnight. Nothing like heaven of course, but darn close. I was alive and home again with my Kal.

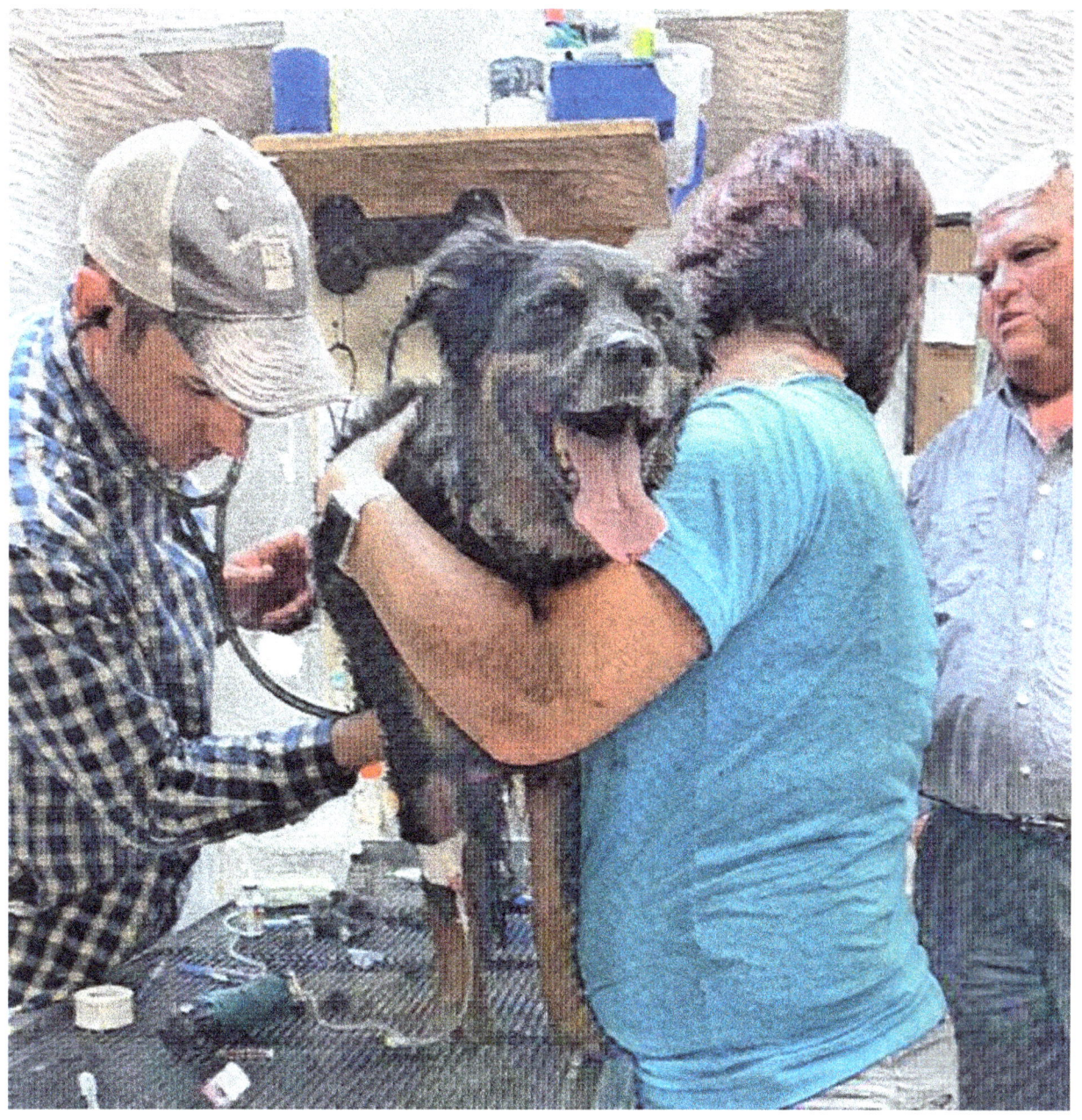

This is me getting a bath after my rescue. It feels so good to have humans take care of me. Of course, they are careful not to get soap in my wound.

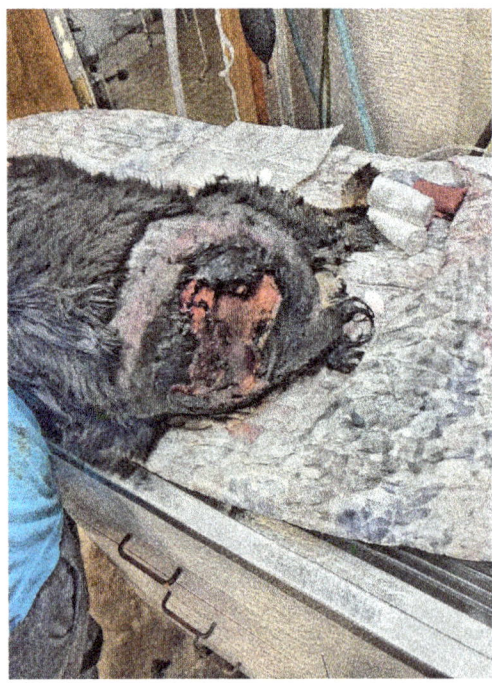

This is my burn wound from the metal contraption.

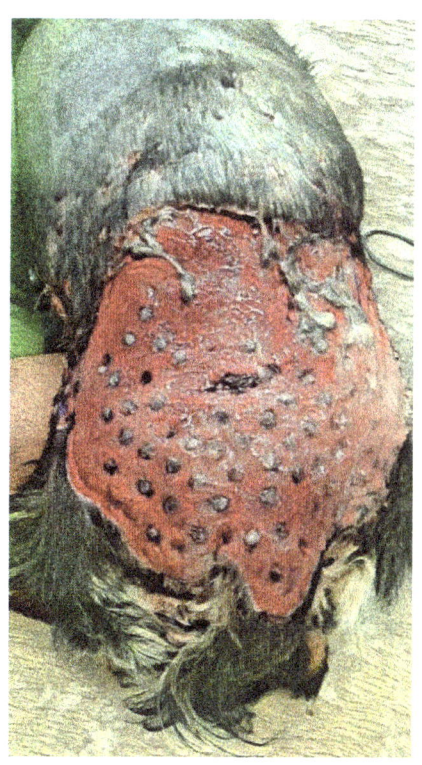

This is my back after surgery. You can see the plugs in my skin.

It took me several weeks to properly heal and several months for my fur to grow back as they had to place plugs in my skin to promote the healing process. It looked like I had a white diaper on for the longest time as the bandaging protected my wounds while I healed. I am now home. *I hate the farm.* And I'm never going back.

But, I am brave because I survived a six day, five night get away, encaged on a metal contraption, with with no food, no water, and a burned rear end. Yes, I am a survivor. I am Brave.

"Come on canine friends. Who wants to go to the farm?" bellows Gramps. Yep! He's at it yet once again!

Are you kidding me? I am staying right here with my buddy Calvin, my cozy bed, and four secure walls to protect me.

Later, gator! I just glare at him with my big brown eyes and don't budge. Thankfully, Grandpa Kevin has learned his lesson and lets me stay behind this time.

This is my buddy Calvin.

ABOUT THE AUTHOR

TAMMY LANE is an elementary teacher with a master's degree in Administration. She is the wife to an amazing husband and father, and the mother of five, of whom are the highlights of her life. Her children range in ages between 10 and 26 and have given her a broad view on the various experiences of children and young adults. She has always loved writing and enjoys reading stories to her children and students. When the opportunity presented itself for this book, she couldn't resist telling this amazing story from both the narrator's and pets point of view. She loves to use life experiences to teach her students and this book is a great way to show how different perspectives can be portrayed from a single event.

CPSIA information can be obtained
at www.ICGtesting.com
Printed in the USA
FSHW02n0209191018
53129FS